Metaphorosis

Apr-Jun 2024

Beautifully made speculative fiction

Also from Metaphorosis

<u>Metaphorosis Magazine</u>

Metaphorosis: Best of 20xx
Metaphorosis 20xx: The Complete Stories
annual issues, from 2016
Monthly issues

<u>Plant Based Press</u>

Best Vegan Science Fiction & Fantasy
annual issues, 2016-2020

from B. Morris Allen:
Chambers of the Heart: speculative stories
Susurrus
Allenthology: Volume I
Tocsin: and other stories
Start with Stones: collected stories
Metaphorosis: a collection of stories

<u>Verdage</u>

Reading 5X5 x3: Changes
Reading 5X5 x2: Duets
Score: an SFF symphony
Reading 5X5: Readers' Edition
Reading 5X5: Writers' Edition

<u>Vestige</u>

The Nocturnals, by Mariah Montoya

<u>Joyful Heave</u>

Museum Piece: an unusual collection

Metaphorosis

Apr-Jun 2024

edited by
B. Morris Allen

ISSN: 2573-136X (online)
ISBN: 978-1-64076-280-0 (e-book)
ISBN: 978-1-64076-281-7 (paperback)

Metaphorosis
a magazine of speculative fiction
from
Metaphorosis Publishing

Neskowin

Apr-Jun 2024

A word about R.W.W. Greene

R.W.W. Greene first came to my attention in 2018, with his story "The Stars Don't Lie" (which we published on 29 June of that year). It's a story about centaurides and magic and fitting in that I really enjoyed.

Greene reappeared in *Metaphorosis* two years later, on 10 July 2020, with a completely different story, "They Build 'Em Tough on Magna Mater", about farm robots repurposed for cage matches.

Both stories have in common a warm humanity concerned with more than just immediate consequences, which is also something you'll find in the next story, "The Wedding of Hope Garrison and Chevrolet Dodge Ford".

The Wedding of Hope Garrison and Chevrolet Dodge Ford

R.W.W. Greene

The farm looked like a lot of them did in them days, one part green to three parts dust. Twenty or thirty head of cattle worked the scrub to the west of the house. Rusted steel slumped on flat, rotting tires. A rickety-looking catfish tank sweated beneath the chicken coop.

The farmer pushed the much-mended baseball cap off his forehead. "How much you charge?"

"Depends," Hank said. "You got power?"

"Some."

"I need 110 to 120. Steady. I can hook my generator in as backup. Only charge you for the fuel."

The farmer took off his cap and wiped his forehead with the back of his arm. "What are we talking in all?"

Hank told him, ignoring the man's wince. "Not every day your daughter gets married, Mr. Garrison. Be a nice surprise for her. Half now. Half after the wedding. Plus meals and a bath."

Farmer Garrison studied his feet a while before tugging his cap back on and sticking out his hand to shake. "You need help setting up? My son knows a thing or two about juice."

Hank jabbed his thumb back at his motorcycle. "Got everything I need right there."

"Lucas!" The farmer hollered, cupping his hands around it. "Lucas!"

A fit young man in patched overalls jogged out from behind the barn. "Yeah, Pa?"

"Walk up and take a look at the water wheel. Make sure the crick's clear and everything's hooked up right." He nodded at Hank. "Man's gonna play music for your sister's wedding tomorrow."

Lucas showed a good set of teeth in his grin. "What's he play?"

"Vinyl," Hank said and tugged the cover off the motorcycle's sidecar. His deejay gear was arranged inside. "Where should I set up?"

The farmer showed him the barn where the reception would be held and helped drag a wooden table into place. "You can plug in there." He pointed to a rusted outlet. "I'll send my daughter in to see ya."

Hank unpacked his turntable and speakers and plugged them into the farm's power. He lifted the crate of records out of the sidecar — about a hundred albums ranging from pristine to warped as hell. He slid the best of the bunch, a copy of Michael Jackson's *Thriller* out of its cover, and lay the needle on side two, track one: "Beat It".

Eddie Van Halen's guitar work filled the dusty barn. According to a book Hank'd owned once, Van Halen's playing was so good the studio caught fire when he laid the riff down. He let the song play. MJ's voice warbled off tempo and key on the second verse. Hank checked the needle and the album for defects. They were perfect. The farmer's power supply was at fault. He ran a line out to the generator in the sidecar.

The record played fine after that, the generator barely a whisper inside the barn. Hank switched on the microphone and leaned in close. "Check. Check. Check," boomed from the speakers. The bride-to-be walked in on the echo.

"Daddy said you're gonna play music for my wedding."

"Best show in town," Hank said. "Get everyone up and moving. Make it a real party."

"Movin' ain't usually a problem with this crowd," she said. "What kind of music you got?"

Her no-color dress was frayed at the hem, and she had wavy hair that would need washing before the ceremony tomorrow. If she were pregnant, it weren't showing.

"Rock 'n roll, ma'am. Country. Mostly late last century." Hank handed her the *Thriller* album cover. The so-called Red-Blue War had left the boundaries of propriety muddy in the 'Messy Middle' states, and there was a chance she'd pitch a fit about being presented with a black man's music. She put the album cover back on the table without comment. "What else you got?" she said.

"Can you read?" He unfolded his catalog carefully and put in on the table.

"Course I can." She tucked her hair behind her ears and bent to puzzle out the list he'd typed out. She bit her lower lip as she traced out the words. Hank would have bet his fee that she hadn't heard anything but live music her whole life, most of that from drunken farmers on broke-down guitars and cigar-box mandolins.

"Do you want some suggestions?" She picked up a record. "He a real prince?"

They spent the next three hours spinning records and picking out her playlist. It was heavy on the Tom Petty, Johnny Cougar, and Bruce Springsteen sort, but she surprised Hank with some of her choices. "Let's Pretend We're Married" off Prince's *1999*. His sole Salt-N-Pepa album, *Hot, Cool & Vicious*, was badly warped, but the last couple of tracks on both sides sounded alright. Hank played "I'll Take Your Man" twice before she scribbled it onto her list. She also showed a fondness for seventies disco and asked him to put "La Freak," "That's the Way (I

Like it)," and "Heart of Glass" in where it felt right.

"What do you want for slow songs?" he said.

"You pick." She fanned herself with the catalog and eyed his stack of records. "You sure got a lot of music."

Hank powered down his gear. "It's just about knowing where to look. Keeping your eyes open."

"Bet you've seen a lot of places."

"Some. Good and bad." The barn was getting warm, and his armpits were uncomfortably damp. "Half and half, I guess."

She sat on the edge of the table. "I ain't been anywhere but here."

And now she was about to get hitched and would likely never get clear. "Here seems nice enough," Hank said.

"It's tiresome. All do this and do that. Wash the clothes. Tend to the chickens. Take care of the kids."

Hank allowed that might get tiresome. "You're getting married."

She folded her arms. "Weren't really my idea. He did the askin'. My step mother said yes, but she ain't the one has to sleep with him."

Hank straightened the stack of records. Once she left, he could put his mind to picking out some slow songs she and her new in-laws might like.

"My name's Hope," she said.

Hank nodded.

"I work hard," she said, "and I'm stronger than I look. I got my letters and numbers. Betcha I could help out at your shows."

"Don't need much help," Hank said. "I got it alright."

"That motorbike of yours is big enough for two. We can pack all this up and be on our way lickety-split." She cocked her hip. "I got money."

"How much?"

She told him.

Not enough. "Sometimes you got to bloom where you're planted, miss."

Hope frowned. Her eyes were near green and life hadn't worn her features sharp yet. Her skin was smooth, except on her hands. She hadn't trued playing pretty yet, but Hank was mostly immune to farmers' daughters anyway.

"I'll do a good job picking out the rest of it, ma'am," Hank said. "It will be a pleasure to hear."

He didn't watch her leave. She might have been serious about running away, or she might have been hoping to see her beau get tough with a wife-stealing deejay. Neither option worked for him. He picked out a dozen or so slow songs, threw in some more fast numbers for the younger women, and typed up the playlist on his portable Royal.

The water pump next to the house ran off an old bicycle, and he had to hunt down the bucket. When he got back to the pump, Lucas met him with a tall glass of lemonade and a plate of food. "Wet your whistle," he said.

"Shouldn't you be getting ready for the rehearsal dinner?"

Lucas sat on the steps and tucked into his own plate. "All I got to do tomorrow is sit and smile. Don't need much practice for that."

The lemonade was cold and sweet. Hank pointed his fork at the pump. "Your doing?"

"Makes things a little easier on my stepmother." He stretched, lean muscles pushing at the fabric of his shirt. "You should let me show you my workshop."

"Got any electrical wire to spare?"

"Might." Lucas took their emptied plates back inside and led the way to a squat blue building on the other side of the house. "Ever see one of these?" Lucas handed him a silver disc from a shelf near the door.

"It's a seedee," Hank said. "Used to put music on them."

"Ever see one work?"

Hank's jaw dropped, half expecting the younger man to wave him over to a working player, but Lucas just laughed. "Me neither." He put the disc back onto the shelf. "Look over here, though." He directed Hank to the far corner of the building. "Nearly got it working."

The thing on the bench was shell-shaped, white on the bottom and translucent orange on the top. A white apple was stenciled on the side. It was attached to a keyboard like the one on Hank's portable typewriter.

"What is it?" Hank said.

"Watch." Lucas tapped the space bar, and a fan came on inside the shell. The glass front lit up and something inside the thing chimed. "Wait for it." A little drawing of an hourglass appeared and flipped over.

And flipped over again. And again. And again.

"That all it does?"

"I get it working all the way, you'll see something!"

"Like what?"

Lucas raised his hands. "Name it. Games. Pictures. Music. Way more than you got. I can get the answer to any question worth askin' once this thing works."

Hank looked at the hourglass. It flipped over again. The screen flickered and went dark. The fan died. Something inside smelled hot. "What are you going to do when you fix it?"

"Sell it, maybe." Lucas grinned. "Buy a motorcycle and get rich making people dance at weddings. You wanna see what I got for wire?"

"Don't really need it." Hank followed Lucas out of the shed. "You really teach yourself all this?"

"Can't spend all my time tendin' the cows." He yawned. "I'm going back up to the house see if they left me any dessert. You?"

Hank shook his head. "Bed. Long day tomorrow."

"Suit yourself." Lucas crooked a half grin. "Holler, you get lonely."

Hank went back to the barn and climbed to the hayloft to sleep. He didn't come awake until he heard the wedding-setup crew stirring in the barn below. He rubbed the sleep out of his eyes and went up to the house to find some breakfast and a bath. The kitchen was full of girls about Hope's age, so he waited until he could flag down someone less likely to want to talk to him. She showed up in a gray dress and a scowl.

"Who you supposed to be?" she said.

Hank offered her his professional bow. "Dancin' Hank, the Wedding Deejay. I'm doing the music for this shindig."

She gave him the eye. "My husband hired you."

"Mr. Garrison and I shook on it yesterday afternoon. Price included meals and a bath."

"He dotes on that girl." She made a face like she'd tasted bad pickles. "You wait here, and I'll get you breakfast. Ask Lucas to show you the crick afterward. That'll do for you."

She ducked into the laughter-filled kitchen and came back out with a plate of beans and bread and a mug of coffee. "Eat it outside. Lucas should be coming back this way in a few minutes."

Hank took the food onto the porch and watched the sun clamber up the sky. Lucas came 'round just as he was sopping up the rest of the bean juice. "Your mama says to show me the crick," Hank said.

"Just about to go down there. Let me get my shave kit, and I'll show ya."

They detoured back to the barn so Hank could get his own kit and the suit he wore for working. Lucas led him away from the house, through the cow field, to a fast-moving stream. He pointed to a shed built over the water. "That's the water wheel. I recoiled the turbine yesterday afternoon so you won't need to tap your generator." He gestured downstream. "It gets deep and wide enough to swim there."

At the edge of the pool, Lucas stripped out of his clothes. His body was lean and strong, with a farmer's tan marking his smooth skin. He smirked, "Last one in's a mama's boy!" and dove in from the shore.

The stream was fresh and cold, and Hank flapped and blew until he got used to it.

"Reckon you're only a year or two older than me," Lucas said.

"Could be," Hank ran his fingers though his sopping hair to tease out the snarls, "but I'm wiser in the ways of the world."

Lucas laughed and play-tackled him, knocking him back into the water. Before Hank knew it, they were splashing each other and wrestling, warm slippery skin on skin. When it got to be too much fun, he pushed away and waded to the shore for his razor. "Got any soap?" he said.

"Over there in my kit." Lucas was floating on his back "Use all you want."

Hank lathered up with the good-smelling soap right there in the stream and rinsed off. He washed his hair and shaved carefully. Lucas watched him the whole time. "What're you looking at?" Hank said.

"Wanted to see if I could learn something new 'bout shaving and washing." Lucas ran his hand over his chest. "But nope. You do it same as me."

Hank toweled off with his dirty shirt. "You'd better get some practice in lest you look a mess for your sister's wedding."

"Think I'd rather float here and watch you."

Hank tried not to dress so fast that he looked nervous. His immunity to farm girls didn't extend to their brothers. He straightened his tie and slid on his shiny, silver jacket. "How do I look?"

"Like the Lord of the Dance hisself." Lucas had come up behind him while he dressed, his voice too close now, his body still cool and wet from the crick. He sniffed the side of Hank's neck. "You smell like me."

Hank cleared his throat. "I better get down there and make sure things are set up right."

"Suit yourself. I'm going back in the water again." Lucas's waist was narrow, his shoulders heavy with work.

"Where'd you learn how to swim so good?" Hank said.

The question stopped the dive back into the stream, as Hank hoped it would. "Hired hand we used to have taught me," Lucas smirked. "Taught me a lot of things." With a flex of leg and buttocks, he dove cleanly into the water.

Hank waited for his head to come up and waved to him. Lucas waved back and stroked away. Hank headed back up the hill.

It was a little too perfect. He might make a move and find himself invited to a game of Kick the Queer. He never won those games. He'd go on his way broke and nursing his wounds, or he'd get run off — still broke — for roughing up a local. Not starting from zero, exactly — he'd done that enough to know the difference — but maybe having to put a pencil line though parts of the map until things cooled down.

Hank wondered if Lucas knew his little sister wanted to cut and run.

The ceremony was set for noon, and Hank wasn't invited, so he went back to the barn to check his rig. He lay his shiny jacket on the table next to his records and spent a few minutes testing the sound again. Six months before and two-hundred miles south, a wire-chewing squirrel had cost him a payday when he dropped the needle on the first song and nothing happened. Hank check-checked the mike and got MJ to tell him to "Beat It" again. He dug a chunk of spruce gum out of his pocket and worked it soft with his teeth.

"Sounds alright." A shadow fell on the turntable. "How'd you hear about us, anyway?"

Cleaned up, Farmer Garrison was a couple of shades lighter. He was tugging on his shirt collar like it wanted to strangle him.

"Store clerk in Franklin," Hank said. "She told me about another wedding to check out next week. 'Bout fifty miles that way." He pointed north. "June and September are my best months."

"You make a living at that?" The farmer's gesture took in Hank's rig. "Showing up to parties and playing old songs?"

"I won't get rich, but yessir. I pick up extra work here and there, too. It suits me. I like to stay on the move."

Garrison nodded slowly. Likely he'd never been much of a traveler. He probably spent his whole life in the same twenty square miles, eyes fixed on a mule's ass. "What's she got you playing?"

Hank fetched the list from his jacket pocket and offered it.

The farmer waved the paper off. "Tell me."

Hank kept an eye on Garrison as he read the list, waiting for the farmer to holler or color up when he got to some of Hope's more scandalous picks. Farmers liked big butts, but they didn't always cotton to songs about them.

"I remember some of those," Garrison said. His face took on a faraway look, and he hummed a piece of something. "My mama used to sing that to my sister."

"Van Morrison's 'Brown-Eyed Girl.' I could sneak it in for you. Make it a father-daughter dance."

The farmer backed away from the table like it had something catching. "It's Hope's party. Let her pick the music. 'Sides," he smiled, "her eyes are green. Like her mama's were."

"Let me know if you change your mind."

He reached to adjust the cap he wasn't wearing. "What's it like out there now?"

Better on the edges than it is here in the middle. Or so I've heard. I've never been all the way west."

Farmer Garrison rubbed his leathery face. "My daddy fought for the Blue. Moved the family out here after. Said it was easier to try to grow your own food than wait in the lines." He looked at Hank sharp. "They still lines?"

"Some places. None of the cities came all the way back. Lot of the ones that didn't have a port emptied out. Others are okay. There's work if you want it. Food. Government has airplanes to move things around now. Trains."

"Lot of people died." Garrison whistled through his teeth. "Lot of people."

Hank didn't bother commenting. When the missiles started flying, both sides gave up claim to the word 'humane', maybe even to 'human'. Then the emps brought everyone back to the early 1900s and left them there.

"I wanted better for my kids, you know?" Garrison reached for his cap again. "Daddy always said he thought we'd get it back together quicker. Teevee, food, electricity for everybody like it grew on trees." He grimaced. "You're probably too young to remember any of that.

"Stories, mostly. Books and magazines."

"Didn't get much of it myself. I was five or six when the grid went down, and we came out here." He drew himself up. "Look at me jawing. Got me a daughter to give away. You know she wanted to be a singer? Talked about it all the time back when she was kid. Not much hope of that now."

The half dozen women still in the barn followed Garrison out the door. "Don't touch anything!" one scolded. They'd decorated with checked tablecloths and streamers and laid the food out on a long table.

Hank put on his shiny jacket and got hisself organized. He cued up the first song Hope'd hear as wife to... what's his name. Hank looked around for a clue to his identity. It would be mighty hard to call a wedding when he wasn't clued in to what to call one half of the happy couple. He finally spotted his name burned into a leather scrapbook on the gift table: "Chevrolet Dodge Ford and Hope Emily Garrison, June 7, 2023."

Hope and Chevy, together forever. A breeze made the tablecloths flutter. The sky darkened. Hank worked another piece of spruce gum soft and popped it into his mouth. It never hurt to have fresh breath.

About thirty minutes later, the ring bearer and the flower girl — the youngest Garrison kids — tore in like the devil was behind them. "Rain's coming!" the girl said. The little boy stuck his finger in the cake.

"Don't!" The girl fetched the boy a clout, and he darted under the table with a finger full of white frosting. The rest of the guests entered at a statelier pace, and Hank powered up the turntable. The B-52's "Love Shack" tumbled out of the speakers. It put the first few folks back on their heels, but the younger people picked up the rhythm and sort of bopped to their seats.

Hank didn't know the groom from Adam, so he kept an eye out for the bride. She entered unsmiling with a dark-haired man whose hairy wrists showed past the cuffs of his jacket. Behind them were Farmer Garrison, his wife, and two beanstalks that had to be the groom's parents.

Hank lowered the music volume and picked up the microphone. "Ladies and gentlemen," he said, "May I introduce Mr. and Mrs. Chevrolet Ford!"

The wedding guests stamped and hooted, and Hank got to work. His hands hummingbirded from record stack to tone arm again and again. Unsleeved vinyl piled up on both sides of him.

The guests tucked into the food and booze. Once in a while, Hank came out and shared some of the dance moves he'd learned from a book his mama had. The Funky Chicken and the Bump. The ladies ate it up and got some of the men to take a nibble, too.

Most of the boys weren't dancing, so Hank got a share of the bounces, flaunts, and coy come-hither looks from the single girls on the floor. He got some play from the married gals, too. Hope leaned low over the table a half dozen times, nearly falling out of her dress, to ask him to play something even faster and wilder. Her face was flushed from the exercise and the pint jar she was waving around. She pushed it into Hank's face. "Drink up," she said. "Can't both of us be sad at my weddin'!"

He told her he was the furthest thing from sad, but she insisted. The shine was bright and clear, almost peppery. He took a long drink and handed it back, sure he'd be flushed and foolish, too, if he had much more. Hope wobbled up on her tiptoes to kiss him on the cheek. She missed, with a little help from her new husband's outstretched hand, and landed on her knees on the floor. Her arm flailed into the turntable. The record needle scraped across three tracks of Tom Petty's "American Girl".

Big, strong Chevrolet Ford stood over his upturned wife, his right hand raised like he was about to slap a mosquito off her cheek. "I knew you wouldn't quit!" he said. "Momma told me you'd never—"

"Nice way to start the honeymoon," Hank said. He could see Chevy Ford was the kind of peckerwood that wouldn't let marriage get in the way of a beating. Hank's stepfather had been one like that.

Chevy shook his fist at him "You shut up, or I'll give you—"

Farmer Garrison hustled over to grab Chevy's arm. "She didn't mean nothing, Chev. She's just happy is all."

Chevy pulled away, nearly toppling his father in-law to the dance floor. "She's nothin' but trash!" He glared at Hope. "All you Garrisons are. Blue State trash."

Farmer Garrison's big right hand shut Chevy up quick. Chevy fell against the table and knocked it over. The turntable bust to pieces on the ground, and Hank's records scattered.

The edge of the table had caught Hank in the chest and knocked the wind out of him. He saw Chevy's pa come up behind

Hope's daddy and rabbit punch him in the neck. Farmer Garrison dropped, and his wife flew at the elder Ford like a wildcat.

The dance floor changed tempo into a brawl. Hank got up and felt his ribs to see if anything was broke. He couldn't breathe so well, but he didn't need air to see the spit and boots flying around the barn. Hank stuffed his records into the milk carton and prodded Hope with his foot. "Let's go," he said, wheezing. "Get your money."

They made it all of fifteen miles down the road before a sharp rock let the air out of Hank's front tire and brought them to a halt. The spare was flat, too.

Hope ran the jack while Hank worked the tire off the rim. One patch didn't do anything to keep the air in, so he tried two. He was up to three patches when the ugliest thing he'd ever seen pulled up behind them. It looked like it might have started life as a pickup truck, but in its death throes it had bedded a tractor and a tarpaper shack.

"Looks like your horse came up lame." Lucas stepped out of the hole where the driver's door should have been. "Might be time to shoot it."

"You here for your sister?"

He shook his head. "Chevy and his pa are looking for her though. Daddy bought us some time by sending them south. He sent me this way."

"Don't suppose you got a new tire in the back of that thing." Hank mopped his forehead.

"Not that will fit, but I got a couple of old turntables we might be able to get working. I hear the job's easier with two. Hope could teach the dancing."

"What about your family?" Hank said.

"Four more where we came from. Step-mother's brood. They'll do alright."

"Maybe you and me will, too," Hank said.

Lucas smiled. "You're getting the right picture now."

The wedding up north wasn't for another week. Time enough to get into one of the abandoned cities and look around for a record shop.

"Help me get my bike on that trailer of yours," Hank said. "We'll all go see if we can find something new to play."

*See R.W.W. Greene's story "The Wedding of
Hope Garrison and Chevrolet Dodge Ford"
online at Metaphorosis.
If you liked it, leave a comment. Authors love
that!
Remember to subscribe to our e-mail updates so
you'll know when new stories are posted.*

About the story

Most weeks during the summer, my spouse and I hold an open-grill event called "Grill Friday". We have the backyard, a cooler, tunes, and the grill. People start showing up at 6 p.m. with a six-pack and something to share. A lot of our people are vegan and vegetarian, so one half of the grill is dedicated to that. A few years ago, a friend was cleaning out her basement, and she brought her ex's record collection along. It had been moldering for years at that point, so I took it upon myself to sort through it and deejay the event with whatever was playable. The story spun up in my head from there. I'm fascinated with the physicality of the older recording methods. You're literally carving the sound into a solid object, and you can get it back out intact as long as you have a needle, an amplifier of some kind, and the right spin speed. We picked up a gramophone recently, and I've been getting it back into working order. It's all springs, gears, and resonators. Not a circuit or power cable to be found. Old tech but once high tech. Maybe high-tech again someday. The rest of the story came out of that.

A question for the author

Q: What is the scariest or most disturbing story you've ever read?

A: The 'man's inhumanity to man' thing always gets me, and one of the best examples of that, in my opinion, is Shirley Jackson's "The Lottery". Just cold, community-supported darkness.

About the author

R.W.W. Greene writes SFF and lives in southern New Hampshire.

www.rwwgreene.com, @rwwgreene

A word about M.E. Bronstein

M.E. Bronstein appeared in the very first year of *Metaphorosis* (20 May 2016), with "Solomon and the Dragon's Tongue", a beautiful story rich with imagery and metaphor. Not only is the final story fantastic (in every sense), it was very good going in. Despite that, during the editing process, Bronstein rewrote the story essentially from scratch — twice! And it just got better and better! Bronstein's been my internal benchmark for hard work and devotion ever since — a near impossible one to match, and one I've tried to apply to my own writing (with far less success).

Happily, she came back to our pages a year later, on 16 June 2017, with "The

Illuminator Leaves", a heartbreaking, but in some ways heartwarming story about the price you pay for art.

Bronstein's brother, Ben, by the way, provided art for three of our covers. Art runs in the family.

Here, Bronstein returns with "Garden Teeth", a story about learning what it is you really want.

Garden Teeth

M. E. Bronstein

Before she died, Ethel gave Julie a stapled packet of parchment paper, plump and noisy with seeds. "For your garden," she said. Julie didn't bother explaining that she lived in a tiny, one-bedroom apartment where she and her husband struggled to keep a box of pansies alive on the windowsill. (And they had only gotten those in the first place because 'pensées' had Charles's favorite double-meaning in French: 'thoughts' as well as 'pansies'.)

They were getting ready for the move — and both Ethel and the pansies had been dead about a year — when Julie rediscovered the seed packet. She tore it open and little yellow-white teeth bounced and clicked across the countertop.

"Oh no-no-no," said Julie, "Goddamnit, Ethel, no."

Julie was a preteen when her mother met Ethel at a women's reading group that formed at shul, and the older woman took the younger under her wing. Ethel started to show up at their apartment some afternoons, and Julie would find the pair of them in the kitchen together, laughing and drinking, Ethel's hand lingering on the seat of her mother's pants; Julie always mumbled an excuse about her homework and went to hide in her room. Ethel interrogated Julie sometimes, checked what she knew about history, literature, and music. She never seemed satisfied, and gave Julie lots of new books to read, which mostly went ignored.

Some days, when Julie's mother realized she'd have to stay late at work, she asked Ethel to pick Julie up from school and watch her for a few hours (or, occasionally, overnight — Ethel first told Julie about the teeth on one such occasion. Back then, Julie assumed that Ethel was just fucking with her).

Ethel was prickly and intense, but there was something mesmerizing in the low urgency of her talk; most of her sentences sounded like little incantations as they flowed out of her. Julie learned that, in her youth, Ethel had been an 'important' (or mildly infamous) scholar, known for her reinterpretations of biblical women — very much a feminist-of-her-moment, all about recuperating literature's Liliths and Delilahs and Jezebels.

Ethel was tall, hair and eyebrows thick and bristling and zebra-striped. She had veins so vivid they almost looked like scars. One flicker of blue forked between her left eyelid and her eyebrow — like lightning, her brain's sparks showing through her skin. She wore heavy jewelry, chunks of stone that clicked and clattered when she moved, a walking billiards table, one piece of her bouncing against another. She could not look motherly, even when doing supposedly nurturing things like cooking. Years later, Julie would retain a vivid mental picture of Ethel: barefoot by the stove in her dressing gown, a cigarette tucked between her lips as she shooed tendrils of smoke and steam out of her gaze and stirred a pot of bubbling purplish-red plum soup. Ethel tipped some leftover wine into the pot, then drank the dregs right out of the bottle.

People asked what Julie would do, when she and Charles went east, and they meant for work; Julie wasn't sure, but she said she'd figure it out. She would not miss her old job. She worked at an immigrant history museum downtown that had been a beautiful Moorish Revival synagogue, built in the late 1800s. When she first got the job she'd imagined she would get to spend more time with the building's crimson carpets, stained glass, the stars painted on the vaults of the sanctuary, but in fact she spent most of her days scheduling tours under the fluorescent lights of the office next door.

So, Julie didn't have much of a 'career' to speak of. She could see herself slipping into domesticity, knew she would become a housewife and occupy herself with the children, tend to the garden. Julie was the only one of her married friends who had taken her husband's last name.

Sometimes, when she talked to old classmates from college and high school, they acted like something was wrong with her, like she should want to be bigger and louder than her own mother had been, and she tried to ignore them.

As she packed for the trip, Julie sewed the teeth into the lining of her jacket. They shifted and settled against her on the way to the airport. She half-expected the metal detectors to keen in response to the strangeness of her cargo, but they didn't. Sometimes she'd put her hand in her pocket and the point of someone's incisor would needle at her fingertip. She felt like a kid with a chick hidden in her clothes, checking to see if it was hungry, cold — did it need anything?

As the plane took off, Julie flipped through her planner. She had a list of things to acquire for the new house. And at the bottom of the list, she regularly wrote, erased, crossed out, and wrote again: *Garden???*

She had scrawled the list on one of several post-it notes that coated the pages of her planner like shingles: to-do lists and shopping lists and various other lists and reminders. Charles leaned his chin on Julie's shoulder and studied Julie while she studied her lists. He said, "What kind of a garden do you want, anyway? Like a vegetable garden? Or something pretty with flowers and stuff?"

"I don't know," said Julie.

"I don't get how you can want a garden and not know what kind of a garden you want."

"I'll know when we get there," said Julie.

"That's not like you," said Charles.

"What do you mean?"

"You like to plan things." He tapped the book in her lap. "Hence the planner."

Julie closed the planner. "I'm throwing caution to the wind. We're going on an adventure. Why not?"

'Adventure' had been Charles's word for it, a way of gentling the sting of temporariness when, after two crushing years on the job market, he had finally given up on his hopes of an immediate professorship and accepted what was a more or less prestigious postdoc in what seemed like a pleasant place. Charles took the book away and laced his fingers through Julie's, clearly relieved that she was trying to see things his way.

After the flight, they got onto a train that would take them into town, and a thin sheen of sweat glittered around Charles's temples as he struggled to hoist their bags up onto the luggage rack. Then he became a sleepy puddle, his sneakers propped up on the seat beside Julie's as she sat opposite him and played with his shoelaces. Light and dark flickered out the window as they emerged from a tunnel, passed trees and telephone poles.

"Charles…"

"Julie?"

"Have I ever talked to you much about Ethel?"

"Your mom's ex? The scary lady who died last year?"

"Yeah. I wouldn't call her 'scary' exactly. There was just something a little — jarring about her." How to say whatever it was she wanted to say? Julie could almost feel the teeth chattering against her skin through the thin cloth of her jacket, trying to speak for her, through her. "She told me the weirdest story once. It was about a family of witches who planted the teeth of their dead like seeds."

"Ick. Why?"

"In the story, the teeth grew into trees and flowers that contained the witches' knowledge and memories."

"They couldn't just write that stuff down? Isn't that what writing is *for*?"

"The women in the story weren't allowed to read or write," said Julie. She asked suddenly, "Have you ever heard a story like that before?"

Charles always knew where stories came from. He thought for a moment, then said, "Well, Cadmus and Jason both plant dragons' teeth, but those teeth don't actually grow into plants; they become people. Then there's that one Brothers Grimm tale — you know, 'The Singing Bone'? One brother kills another and buries him beneath a bridge, but his bone sings, 'My brother killed me'."

"Hmm. But that's about brothers. This one is about sisters. And mothers and daughters and grandmothers."

"I'll look into it, if you like. But I'm not sure I'll find a clear or exact source — maybe it was something Ethel just made up? Anyway, did anything in particular make you wonder about this?"

"I don't know. I just catch myself thinking about her sometimes, since she died." She reached for a reason he would understand. "She wanted to be remembered and I'm not sure anyone will remember her except me."

Charles leaned forward, pressed Julie's fingers in his. "I'll look into it," he said again. "You said she was sort of a scholar, right? Maybe she wrote about this story."

Julie nodded, though that seemed unlikely. Something about the story had felt very private and secret when Ethel told it to Julie.

"Listen," said Ethel, "there's a story I should tell you."

Julie tried to figure out a way to tell her she wasn't *that* little (like seriously, she was twelve), and she didn't need a bedtime story or whatever. Ethel settled at the foot of her bed anyway and tried to figure out a way to begin and Julie let her because she didn't know how to ask her politely to leave.

At last, Ethel found her way into her story: "Once, there was an old woman who lived in a big house with her daughters and granddaughters. People don't like women who live in big houses all together, especially when they have sharp teeth, which these women did. Their neighbors spread rumors that the old woman and her daughters and granddaughters put on snakeskin at night and slithered through town biting people, poisoning them as they slept. And this wasn't the first time people had said things like that about these women; the old woman had run away and started over in many, many different places over the course of her youth and she was getting tired of it. She and her daughters were never allowed to learn how to read or write. People were afraid of what they would do if they could write things down.

"Anyway, during the old woman's final years, two of her daughters died. I don't know if people killed them, or if they just died of some combination of hunger and sickness. Anyway, the old woman's youngest granddaughter noticed that as her aunts died, new flowers appeared in their garden. And the old woman explained to her, 'Your aunts are not truly dead. They are still here. They can still speak to us.'

"One day, the old woman gave her granddaughter instructions to go foraging in the woods, and she told her she should not come back for three days. The granddaughter asked why, and her grandmother wouldn't tell her. But the granddaughter was dutiful; she did as she was told, and when she returned home, she found everything broken and blackened; their neighbors had burned the house and garden down. The granddaughter remembered what her grandmother had told her, that her aunts could speak through the flowers. She worked around her tears and picked through the ashes of the garden, searching for at least one petal that might have survived. Instead, she found three teeth.

"She hid the teeth in her boot and spent many years drifting as her grandmother once had,. Some strangers who didn't know any better would take her in and let her work in their kitchens, their barns, until something crept out of her that frightened them: a glimpse of teeth just a little sharper than most people's are. And then she would run away again.

"Eventually, she found a little village where she kept her mouth shut and didn't bother anyone, and so her neighbors grew accustomed to her and let her be. She settled in a hut with a patch of dirt where she grew a new garden. And she collected a couple of beggar girls and made them her daughters.

"The granddaughter (now a mother) planted her family's three teeth, and they grew into a mulberry, a willow, and a fig tree. Sometimes, when she listened to their leaves, she heard whispers, but they never amounted to anything meaningful. But when she tore a switch from her willow and stirred her stews with it, or when she drank tea made of the mulberries and fig leaves, she started to understand; her garden gave her verses, rhymes, stories, prayers. In a nutshell: knowledge.

"And the granddaughter became an old woman in turn, and she remembered old spells and poems, and spoke in others' voices, in riddles. Once, she hadn't been allowed to read; later, she was too busy moving and surviving to learn; now, at last, she had time, but she was too old and tired. She never learned and so never taught her daughters. She decided it didn't matter; they had their gardens instead.

"And one day, she told her eldest granddaughter, 'When I die, you must pluck the teeth from my skull and plant them in your own garden.'"

Ethel watched Julie for a reaction. Julie said, "Gross."

An old friend of Charles's had worked for a few years as a lecturer at the university, but since he had at last managed to snag a tenure-track job at a small college upstate, Charles and Julie inherited his townhouse at the edge of campus. The situation was far from luxurious (the floors linoleum, the walls peppered with the scars of previous occupants' nails and thumbtacks and the inverted shadows left by their posters), but it was still more space than Julie had ever been able to pretend ownership of since she started calling herself an adult. Charles's friend left a faded aroma of lavender and gin in his wake. In spite of the bright summer weather, it always felt chilly as a cave indoors, no matter how much Julie fiddled with the thermostat, and she often walked around beneath a heap of blanket.

About a week after their arrival, they were having their breakfast together in the new kitchen, Julie stirring instant coffee that smelled like dog food. Charles had a fat book out on the table, and Julie peered over his shoulder. It took her a moment to process the author's name at the top of the page: Ethel Milgrom. Her attention darted down the page:

Lilith makes a sideways, skittering appearance in Isaiah 34:13-14:

'And thorns shall come up in her palaces, nettles and brambles in the fortresses thereof: and it shall be an habitation of dragons, and a court for owls. The wild beasts of the desert shall also meet with the wild beasts of the island, and the satyr shall cry to his fellow; the screech owl also shall rest there, and find for herself a place of rest.'

The English I've just provided is from the King James Bible (venerable standard and monolith that it is). But you might notice that something is missing. Where, oh where is Lilith? I promised we would find her here.

I'll tell you: she's hiding (she does that). The KJV's 'screech owl' replaces the Hebrew 'lilit'. The Vulgate Latin likewise dances around Lilith and dubs this mysterious creature the 'lamia'. And so we have two phases of erasure, in Latin and in English.

Ever since, Lilith has hidden in various literary corners. In accordance with this pattern, I read her as hidden in Keats's

Lamia; *picture her, coiled underground (under the page), waiting …*

And then there was more stuff about the Keats poem, which didn't mean much to Julie, since she had never read it.

There were two pictures reproduced in black-and-white on the verso: Dante Gabriel Rossetti's *Lilith*, brushing her lustrous heap of hair, and John William Waterhouse's *Lamia*, on her knees before her unsuspecting knight, crumpled snakeskin hidden in a corner of the scene.

"I've been looking into Ethel's work," said Charles needlessly. "I haven't found anything about teeth yet, but it appears dear old Ethel had a serious thing for Lilith. And other snaky-demonic temptress ladies who eat children and lure silly men to their deaths."

"And what do you think? Of Ethel's work?"

"Oh — it's interesting? Entertaining? This fever-dream kind of theorizing isn't really my style, I guess. I'm a stodgy and traditional researcher and I like my clear and explicit arguments and evidence, thank you very much. I don't really get this stuff that was in fashion a few decades ago where you can almost smell the weed on the pages. But you should read and see for yourself."

Julie almost laughed; she knew already it would hurt to follow the windy path of Ethel's thought through her early-morning brain fog. "Maybe later," she said.

She stepped toward the sliding door beyond the kitchen table, and it stuttered on its track as she shoved it. She hovered on the threshold and let a breeze twine around her hair and ankles. Much more rousing than the coffee. Charles came to her side and they studied the lawn: a little stretch of grass with a chain-link fence around its perimeter. There was a big planter box with a pale wooden frame, poorly sanded and ready to give them splinters.

"Well?" said Charles. "What's it going to be? Vegetables or flowers or rocks or sculpture? That should about cover all possible gardeny things, right?"

"Flowers," said Julie.

Charles agreed, "Flowers."

The bedroom Julie sometimes occupied at Ethel's had clearly belonged to another girl once. Someone about her age, maybe a couple years younger — but precocious, smarter than Julie. Julie felt around the sharp edges of an old tragedy, which explained something about the way Ethel looked out of windows on rainy mornings, as though willing the day to complete itself. The meaningless tasks she gave herself: scrubbing already-clean surfaces, disentangling old skeins of yarn she would not use anyway, sifting through lentils and picking out the brown and pebbly ones. The kinds of tasks an evil stepmother would assign her stepdaughter, but Ethel was the stepdaughter and stepmother in one very garbled package.

Asking about the other girl would be wrong, invasive. And yet Julie kept running into pieces of the room's shadow occupant. She found ancient and moon-pale pads of gum wadded on the underside of the desk. There were bright scraps of tissue paper glued to the window in a child's facsimile of stained glass, so that looking outside meant looking through the wing of a giant, demented butterfly, all patchwork crimson, teal, and amber.

Julie benefitted from the yellowing paperbacks left on the room's shelves and got to know her predecessor's handwriting in the margins. The two of them were often at odds with each other. The other girl disliked quietness. Julie wanted to write a retort whenever she found a frowny face in a book's margins. The other girl wrote *boring* a lot when authors waxed too descriptive and went on about landscapes or architecture.

I don't believe you, thought Julie, one eye on the colorful window. Whoever she was, the other girl had been in the habit of wishing herself elsewhere — even if she didn't like to admit it. Julie could feel her restlessness brined in the room's murky light.

Julie was not a natural gardener. Once, in her early twenties, her uncle had trusted her with housesitting while he was on vacation, and she killed his potted geraniums and spider plant with over- and under-watering respectively.

Not that being a decent gardener mattered much. The flowers were just a big and showy thing to distract potential naysayers from her real project: the teeth. Still, Julie bought a pile of gardening books and looked up whatever was seasonal and local and more or less straightforward to take care of. Which meant flowers with names that sounded like they belonged to debutantes in pearls and silk gloves: dahlias, peonies, clematis.

They went to a nursery and collected dahlias with fat pink and orange heads. It turned out they had plump tuberous roots, and Julie wondered if you could eat them like potatoes and parsnips. Fleshy, mandrakish. Julie read that they liked bone meal. She roasted a chicken, picked the fat off its bones, boiled them clean. She turned the bones brittle in the oven before wrapping them up in a plastic bag, and when she smashed them with a meat tenderizer, Charles ran in to check that she wasn't murdering someone.

Later, Julie sprinkled bone dust into holes in the planter box's soil, hefted the flowers and set their tubers gingerly in place. Each time she did so, she'd glance back at the house, the windows, to check if Charles was watching her — he sometimes did, amused by the spectacle of her and dirt, which did not ordinarily go together.

Her husband's absence confirmed, Julie would slip a tooth out of her pocket and put it into the earth before she planted a dahlia to guard it.

Some of the flowers needed to lean on stakes to hold their fat heads upright. Once she had planted about five of them, Julie stood back and admired the effect. Her radiant and crooked children.

Meanwhile, Charles occupied an office at the university and made friends with a handful of new colleagues. Once they had settled in sufficiently and cleaned the house, he invited them over for dinner, and they discussed university politics; Charles compared 'back home' and here. Julie wasn't sure why he kept calling the other place 'home' when it seemed unlikely they would go back. She made ratatouille for dinner with a colorful array of tomatoes from the farmers' market, and Charles's new colleagues praised her cooking and asked what she did, which Julie and Charles jointly deflected by making jokes about the garden, it being Julie's new 'project'. They took their guests to the yard, where they shivered in the early evening chill. Twilight burnt the deep blue sky orange at the edges, early stars and satellites blinked above the trees' shivering silhouettes, and the little dahlias looked very squat and simple next to that.

"My Lilith," said Charles, one hand on her shoulder.

"Who?" said Julie. "Me? What? No. What do you mean?"

He said, " 'The rose and poppy are her flowers.' "

Rossetti. "No-no," said Julie. "Away with you. No roses or poppies here."

"In spirit."

"Not in spirit. Dahlias. Dahlias in actuality."

"That's harder to fit into iambic pentameter."

Julie got self-conscious then, especially because of the bright and promising young professor who'd asked what she did in the first place, and the way she squinted at Julie, and Julie could almost hear her thinking, So, *she cooks* and *gardens*, as she checked Julie's back for a wind-up key.

Julie pressed her shoulder blades against the house's clapboard walls.

She listened and listened. Not to Charles and his new colleagues — who talked about Rossetti, Keats, poets and painters and their flowers — but to the garden.

Waiting, always waiting, for it to start talking.

One day, Ethel unearthed a cigar box hidden behind old, dark bottles of whisky and amaro in the liquor cabinet.

Inside the box were several little muslin bags, each tied shut with a pale string. Ethel took one of the bags out and handed it to her. Julie loosened its opening and carefully spilled some of its contents into the palm of her hand.

There were bits of dried flower, fragrant and brittle. And a few shriveled pods. It all smelled like earth and roses and decay.

Ethel gestured for Julie to give the bundle back to her. She transferred its contents into a tea ball, which she submerged in a mug of hot water.

She gave it to Julie. "Drink," she said.

Julie hesitated. She remembered the story. The granddaughter who stirred her witches' brews with willow wands and nibbled like a silkworm on mulberry leaves, and was changed by what she consumed.

"Drink," said Ethel, and Julie didn't know how to get around the clear note of command. The tea was still very hot and it burned her tongue. She waited, terrified, expecting to croak, for toads and snakes to fall out of her mouth like the wicked girl in that one fairy tale.

Ethel watched her until she drank the whole mug of tea, then took it from her and dropped it in the sink amid a mounting pile of dirty dishes.

Julie kept waiting. But nothing happened, and that almost disappointed her.

That is, nothing happened until much later — a few days after drinking the remains of some old garden of Ethel's (or Ethel's grandmother, who knew?), Julie was in her English class, staring at a pop quiz, and at first she couldn't remember what 'ossify' or 'nacreous' meant, but then it came to her. Not only that, but she knew both words' Latin roots, even though she'd never studied Latin.

Later, Julie poked around corners of her memory and discovered fragments of other languages. And stories. And spells and riddles.

In her dreams, she smelled flowers and her teeth were sharp as thorns.

The dahlias had been in place about a week when they started to wither. Pink petals turned orange, then brown, and curled into themselves. Julie thought of dead spiders with their legs coiled into their abdomens, salted leeches, burning paper.

Their heads drooped. Every single one.

Charles said maybe something underground was lunching on their roots. He suggested pesticide and Julie said no.

The first weeds appeared a few days after the dahlias died.

Julie made no connection between the weeds and the teeth at first. The books had informed her: look out for weeds, they will sneak in.

Julie tore out creeping, twining threads of green and brown and their little leaves. They kept coming back. Some weeds she knew (buttercups, clover, groundsel), others she didn't. She took pictures and sifted through her books. Corncockle and feverfew and chickweed. They looked innocuous, pretty even — little purple and white flowers, tiny and starry. But then they spilled out of the planter box and spread through the yard.

The garden knotted, tangles of color resurging almost as soon as Julie eradicated them. When she retreated to the kitchen and guzzled a glass of water, Charles held her face, rubbed at a smear of soil on her cheek and said she looked like she had come back from a fight with a dragon —

And then something clicked.

Dragons, serpents, lamias. Witchy, snaky women with sharp and needling teeth.

It all felt so much like a trick they would play. She gave them a home and they gobbled up her dahlias.

Could it be? She couldn't confirm without digging and inspecting the teeth to see if they had burst open and all this life had started crawling out of them. And Julie couldn't do that, wouldn't upset or disrupt them.

That evening, she woke up after midnight. Charles didn't stir as she crept out from their sheets, tugged on a sweater, slunk downstairs, to the yard, shivered and studied her handiwork. Hoped to catch the teeth in the act overnight, when they didn't expect her.

And then, a strange call — low and hollow. It stretched out and then stuttered, repeated after itself. Probably just an owl. They had weird calls out here. There was one species that locals said chanted, "Who-cooks? Who-cooks-for-yooouuu?"

And Julie might have accepted that it was just an owl, might have gone inside again, if not for the yellow flowers.

It could have been a trick of the gloom and starlight, that they seemed to glow and pulse, flower heads that had been closed for the night opening to peer at her. And Julie stepped backward, hovered on the threshold. In another frame of mind, she'd have laughed at herself. Quaking before a bunch of glinting weeds.

She retreated, hand rattling as she slid the door shut and locked it, like the weeds would creep in after her if she wasn't careful. She went back to bed and wondered if Charles would notice when he woke up that they had new neighbors, a little coven of dandelions that hadn't been there the day before. Weedy lions' teeth bristling out of the earth.

After Ethel made her drink the tea, the voices stayed in Julie's head for maybe a couple of weeks, and then they faded and Julie became herself again. The scraps of language and knowledge she'd imbibed got lost somewhere. And so Julie resumed being Julie, a mediocre student, listless and inclined to stare at the window instead of listening to the teacher.

Julie thought about asking Ethel for more of her tea. She could feel Ethel waiting for her to ask for more.

In a really stupid way, the voices that had traveled from the dried leaves and petals into her brain had been her only friends, these past few months. The only people who really paid attention to her — not like the girls she ate lunch with in the cafeteria, who only ever wanted to talk about bad pop groups and parties Julie hadn't been invited to.

But those little voices whispering at the back of Julie's head had scared her, too. Their attention sometimes felt hungry, desperate. Like wayward mountain lions, coyotes, hunting for chickens in their neighbors' backyards.

One lingering memory explained the underlying principle: that a tooth's fruit could be tamed and tempered a little; a flame and boiling water could cook just a little of the voice out of it so that it would sit in her gut without devouring or clamoring over her. So, Ethel had been protecting her, by giving her a taste of the garden-as-tea; that made consuming the garden a little safer. But still: the threat of being overtaken. It was there.

They had lain dormant for a long and lonely time.

Julie had been old enough by then that her mother trusted her more on her own. She stopped asking Ethel to look after Julie, who didn't see Ethel for months at a time. Though sometimes her mother still gave Julie books and said they were from Ethel, and Julie would open them up and pressed flowers would fall out from between the pages and into her lap. She flushed them down the toilet.

Dandelions' yellow and white heads dotted the planter box and the surrounding grass, a lacy froth of petal and pappus. The planter box had turned into an overflowing pool of weeds — greens and tawny golds, shocks of purple and white and yellow — that spilled out and softened the boundary between the box and the rest of the yard.

Charles approved. "The other flowers — what were they again, dahlias? — that was all wrong, I see it now. Manicured, artificial. This feels... wilder. More natural. It's pretty."

But he only said that because he couldn't hear them.

Not that Julie could, either, really. But she almost could. Maybe they had been quiet for so long, they'd forgotten how to talk, and so they couldn't communicate in any identifiable language — but there was an intensity about the garden, a ghost of noise, like a faraway growl of thunder, an itch buried deep in Julie's skull. She gathered dandelions, tucked them into her hair, arranged them in mason jars and left them to wilt on the kitchen table. She kept them nearby. She listened.

And still they wouldn't talk.

Later, Julie wouldn't be sure what took her so long, why she hesitated.

One day, she had spread a picnic blanket in the yard and had a sunhat on and lounged with a magazine in her lap. Some of the flowers were heavier than they should've been, their petals brittle. Almost like they were tiny, very accurate sculptures of flowers, rather than the real thing.

Julie closed her book and plucked a pale globe of dandelion. She twirled its waxy strand of stem between her fingertips. She tried not to fidget it to death, but it still shed feathery seeds across her lap. She listened.

The dandelion has many uses. Its petals can produce a delicate yellow dye. It's also been called piss-a-bed (after its French name, pissenlit) because of its diuretic value. It can soothe troubled stomachs and teeth. But to most of us, it's an invader, bright and annoying. So, what else would Ethel's child choose, to grow out of her soul's soil? It had to be her.

Julie remembered that if you consume the fruit of garden teeth thoughtlessly, it will eat you up from the inside out, sprout out the top of your skull and speak its own poetry.

And then she ate the dandelion's head off. She gagged a little (it tickled).

It chattered as it fell through her.

She remembered that some people believe the dandelion's airborne seeds are like will-o-the-wisps, souls of the dead drifting on the wind.

Even after Ethel and Julie's mother grew apart, they still talked a lot, and Ethel always asked how Julie was doing and still sent her too many damn books (no more flowers pressed into them, though, like maybe, just maybe, she was conceding defeat on that front). Julie visited her a handful of times over the course of her adult years.

The very last time Julie saw Ethel before she died, Ethel had covered the windows up with heavy curtains and lived in the dim, and Julie caught herself tiptoeing around patches of molten light that slipped inside, like she'd burn herself on them if she weren't careful.

Ethel brusquely swept coats and old skeins of yarn off the couch before she let Julie sit, then brought out a tarnished tray cluttered with old porcelain. She stirred her tea with a silver spoon even though she hadn't put honey or anything in it.

Ethel said, "You're grown up now."

"I don't feel very grown-up," said Julie mechanically.

"And you're married?

"Yes," said Julie. She rushed to add, "If there had been a real wedding we would have invited you. Charles was busy, and neither one of us wanted it to be a big thing, so we just went to the courthouse with a couple of friends for witnesses."

Ethel nodded and sipped her tea. "Little Julie," she said. "I can't believe it."

And Julie showed her pictures from the courthouse — half to prove the truth of what she'd said. It was nice at least to talk to someone about it who wouldn't probe about her husband or ask if he meant to convert (not that Julie's mom gave a damn, but too many aunts and uncles did). Julie had worn a short-sleeved dress, pale champagne silk. Julie told Ethel about Charles. "You'd like him," she said.

"I'm sure you'll be very happy," said Ethel, as if the prospect bored her. "Cheers." She startled Julie then by asking when they would have children. She didn't ask *if* they wanted children, but *when* — as though the children in question were an expected infestation, like cicadas, and Ethel had only forgotten where they were in the cycle, how many years were left until they swarmed aboveground again.

"That's kind of a personal question, Ethel."

"Can't I ask you kind of personal questions?"

"I guess. Well, the answer is, I don't know. Soon. Before long."

And then, Ethel startled Julie again by talking about her own daughter.

"We used to have a garden," said Ethel. Her daughter used to dig holes in it. She said she was digging a well. She'd come inside and fill a plastic bucket with water, take it out (sloshing all over the place), fill the hole she'd dug, then would get upset when the water just faded into the earth, and it darkened and softened.

She loved dandelions, but only after they'd turned pale and feathery, and she'd breathe them to pieces. (She didn't know that some people think dandelions are prophetic: blow and then count the leftover seeds, and you will learn how many years you have left to live.) She loved the buttercup game but always held them too close to her chin and crushed them.

Ethel's daughter spent less and less time in the garden as she grew up. Ethel had been trying to think about ways to entice her back into the garden when —

well, you know. Forcing her would have backfired anyway; she was the kind of daughter who would scream and squirm if made to do anything she hadn't decided on herself.

They shook hands as Julie left. Ethel's fingers felt so small and dry, but she clutched Julie's hand so tightly, her heavy rings became signets, marking Julie's skin like wax.

The dandelions grew and spread beneath Julie's skin.

Julie and Charles were getting ready for bed, hovering around the sink as they brushed their teeth. Charles spat and stared at Julie, and she said, "What?"

He reached and touched her throat; his fingertips traveled, traced her collarbones. Julie studied herself in the mirror, tugged at her nightshirt to better see the skin of her neck and chest, and she found a sequence of yellowish patches: dark at the center, a starburst around the edges. Something between a bruise and a flame caught beneath her skin.

"How'd that happen?" said Charles.

"I'm not sure," said Julie. "Must have been while I was gardening."

"It looks like someone threw rocks at you or something."

"Yes, the neighbors come and stone me when you're not around," said Julie, then regretted joking when Charles's mouth flattened. She had buried herself in gardening, hadn't started to look for work or any foothold in the local 'community'. What was the point, when they would just leave in a couple of years anyway, when Charles went on the job market again? Putting down roots felt foolish. The dahlias had taught her the illogic of that.

"It's probably some kind of rash," said Julie. "An allergic reaction. I must have touched something funny in the garden, then scratched myself."

It didn't hurt or burn or itch, though.

Charles nodded, gnawed his lower lip, visibly chose to believe her — for now. The dark way he studied her through lowered eyelashes said he'd check soon whether or not the mysterious bruises faded or lingered, and Julie found herself strategizing already, mentally picking out turtlenecks to wear that lay buried at the bottom of tightly taped boxes of winter clothes they hadn't even bothered unpacking.

The next day, Julie went to the farmers' market and came back with a basketful of plums, which she cut in half and pitted, and Charles came home and looked over her shoulder at her bubbling pot of purple and said, "Oh my, a witch's brew!"

"A recipe from the Old Country," joked Julie — and only then realized that it was Ethel's recipe, not something she'd grown up with herself. She said that plums were in season, and he asked if she needed help, and when of course she didn't, he set up his books on the table and kept up whatever work he'd started earlier in the day at the university.

While Julie leaned over the pot and its steam curled up in her hair, he spoke.

He said, "What's that?"

"What's what?"

"That tune," he said.

"Tune?"

"You were whistling something," he said. He considered, then added, "I don't think I've ever heard you whistle before."

And now that he'd interrupted, Julie could feel the song leaving her lips, but could not for the life of her retain whatever it had been.

Julie forgot to answer sometimes when Charles said, "Julie? Earth to Julie?" She forgot, again and again, that that was her name. It had gotten lost somewhere in the petals she gathered and sugared, then mixed into her oatmeal.

She went foraging in the woods near campus for yellow chanterelles (she knew where to find them now) and didn't come home until midnight, her forearms scratched and bruised.

She dipped a needle in ink and drove it into the flesh of her thigh because she remembered an old design that used to live there — a stylized dog rose — and she missed it, knew it had kept her safe.

They had the same conversation over and over. Charles said things to the effect of *You're making me nuts. Are you trying to make me nuts? Are you trying to punish me for taking you away?*

But he hadn't 'taken' her anywhere — she had come because she wanted to. Julie had followed him, because that was Julie's thing. To find someone to trail after, because she didn't know what to do with herself otherwise.

He had asked many times if she was okay with it.

"I know, I know," said Julie.

She hadn't been happy, back west. Or that was how Charles put it. News to her — but she got what he meant. She hadn't been thriving.

"And you thought I would do better here?" she said. In new soil? Did he think the fresh, different air would clean the shadows out of her brain? (She giggled, and Charles said, "Are you *laughing*?" And she said, "No I'm giggling.")

He had been thinking of their future, the family they were planning, and they needed money, he needed to have something resembling a career to realize their plans, since Lord knows Julie wasn't showing much motivation in that regard, and that should have made Julie angry, but it didn't. She thought of Ethel. Perhaps Ethel had in fact chosen her because of her dullness and normalcy. All Julie wanted was a family, and so she would give the teeth daughters to talk to, and more teeth to put underground in turn.

Charles said, "I just want you to be happy. Please tell me what will make you happy."

Then it rained and rained and Julie sprouted a fever and Charles took care of her, brought her tea and pressed wet towels to her forehead. He stayed home from the university and lingered by her side.

Julie could not remember smelling things in her dreams before the teeth. But now bursts of perfume and musk wafted through her sleep. Pretty scents like jasmine, honeysuckle, rosemary, but also the dry-erase funk of soft brown apples, cherries, plums melting and fermenting in sticky puddles of sloughed off skin.

And she heard whispers.

The lamia, the serpent in the garden, sows her own teeth to grow a garden of memories.

If you hear your child laughing at you know not what, perhaps your little girl has devoured the fruit of some witch's garden teeth, and you must touch her nose and intone, "Out, Lilith!"

(If you want Lilith out, that is.)

Once there were a grandmother, a mother, and a daughter. When the grandmother died, the mother sowed her tooth, which grew and became an apple tree, and the good and dutiful daughter ate an apple, and so the grandmother took root in her granddaughter and spoke out of her mouth.

When the mother died, the granddaughter sowed her teeth, which became a blackberry bush, and she fed blackberries to her own daughter in turn.

You see how this goes. A pattern, an unending braid of the same three women, over and over. Eating, becoming, birthing each other.

Apples and blackberries and and and.

Cloves or maybe clematis or cardamom.

Around goes the daisy chain.

Sometimes, a young girl slipped through Julie's dreams. About nine or ten years old. A flash of dark hair, wavering behind a tree. Playing hide-and-seek. Julie stepped toward her; a branch snapped beneath her weight. The child giggled and lurched away. She ran uphill, and Julie followed her.

She was losing her, the girl going too fast.

Julie wanted to call after her, demand that she stop. But she couldn't. She touched her own mouth, pried her lips apart. Pulled on her tongue to make sure it was still there.

"Rose!" she called, because that, it turned out, was the girl's name.

And Rose stopped. She had led Julie to a clearing in the middle of the forest with a house in it. An ugly, squat little gray building, but surrounded by a colorful and very weedy gated garden. The gate was open and Julie stepped through.

The garden was full of dandelions and bees and flies and life. It turned out to be much more expansive than it had seemed from just outside the gate. Tall grasses brushed against Julie's skirt, thorns prickled against her skin. She followed an avenue between densely gathered shrubs and low trees with twisting branches. The scene darkened as she got lost in it, the swampy green dim interrupted only by starbursts of dandelions. Behind her, Rose said,

How to entangle, trammel up and snare
Your soul in mine, and labyrinth you there
Like the hid scent in an unbudded rose?

They took one turn, then another, and another. Julie realized she wouldn't be able to make her way out of this place again without Rose's help. The girl laced her fingers through Julie's and led her deeper into the maze of trees and dandelions, and Julie let her.

When she woke at last, Julie stayed languid and clumsy. She kept knocking things over by accident and cut the soles of her feet on broken glass. When Charles suggested they make a doctor's appointment, she insisted no, she was all better, she just needed time to find her legs again, and she did not tell him that there were a few minds stuffed into her head beside her own now, and they weren't used to the weight and length of her body.

She fell back into the rhythm of her life, more or less. Except she kept getting that life just a little wrong as she forgot how to put on an accurate performance of 'Julie'. The Julie Charles knew always complained about the cold and kept the windows shut; the unbudded rose in Julie kept opening the windows and letting flies and wasps and moths inside. Charles hated things that tasted like licorice, and Julie knew that, and yet she kept putting caraway and anise in their food. She forgot to turn the gas off, and Charles shook her and said, "Jesus, Julie, wake up! Where the hell is your head?"

How to explain that she was just filling in the gap of a young girl's death? While the other women faded in and out of her, Julie had given Rose a permanent maze to hide in. And it was frightening to realize how much she liked that, liked dissolving, becoming someone else, someone more important than Julie.

Charles suggested again and again that Julie look for work in the area, even though his stipend was generous enough to support them both; he didn't like all the time she was spending alone (he didn't know that she wasn't *really* alone).

Julie had an old necklace of Ethel's with a chunk of jasper for a pendant: striped orange, polished and cool in her hand. She gathered henbane from the garden, purple veins crackling through its white petals. She made a nest of flowers in a bowl, laid the jasper at its center like an egg, and Charles slept very soundly that night. He woke up later and more slowly than usual, smiled foggily at Julie. He kissed her forehead and left her to her gardening.

As autumn came and the garden wilted, Julie wrapped bouquets of dandelions in twine, pressed buttercups between the pages of Charles's books, sealed nettles and mallow blossoms in jars. She brewed teas and broths and sifted through thoughts that weren't hers.

She had a faint recollection of pliers, cotton, a little plastic bottle of rubbing alcohol. And blood on white porcelain, fading to pink as it mixed with water.

Ethel, tugging out one of her own teeth before she died.

Faded memories of her mother came and went, too: how Julie's mom stared at Ethel with wide eyes, how she called her 'brilliant' and 'sharp', like she was a sunrise or a cliff face, not a woman, even though sometimes, all Ethel really wanted was to be soft and muted with someone.

Charles started to apply to jobs again. Last time he had gone through this process, he asked Julie's advice, made her read his dossiers, probably just so she felt involved even though she didn't always understand the point of his work.

This time, however, she became much more interested. She scribbled questions in the margins of his writing samples. She dashed off check marks when Charles said something surprising or creative. She wrote *boring* when he went on too much and made basically the same point over and over. Charles laughed and said, "Harsh. But okay, I see what you mean."

Julie whispered to the dried garden by moonlight, and offers came in the spring as the garden bloomed again.

They started to talk more about the things they used to dream up together. They talked about children. What they would call their daughters. They talked about these things even when the henbane and jasper started to wear off, and Charles looked at her so warily sometimes, like he didn't recognize her. Julie knew his uneasy sense that she wasn't (quite, or just) the person he'd married would slowly push them away from each other, the way creeping weeds and ivies can become part of a wall and then dismantle it.

Sometimes Julie felt her canines with her tongue and imagined that they were just a little bit sharper than they used to be. Or maybe that was Rose, crawling on all fours beneath the dining table, pretending she was some kind of wildcat. When Ethel peered down at her, Rose hissed, and Ethel said, "What the hell are you up to, you crazy kiddo?"

Julie remembered Ethel (she remembered *being* Ethel), her pen starring the page as she hunted for signs of Lilith in Keats's *Lamia: Her throat was serpent, but the words she spake / Came, as through bubbling honey, for Love's sake.* Ethel, who mixed and muddled her literary interpretations with biblical apocrypha and kabbalistic sources, noticed that the *Zohar* described Lilith in rather similar terms: it compared her tongue to a sword, her words to oil, her lips to roses full of sweetness. Ethel saw kinships between all these women with lions' teeth, snakes' skin, and owls' wings, who lurked in forests and gardens and swamps.

Julie remembered being Ethel, sitting at the edge of Rose's bed, and then Julie's, telling her a story. And Julie remembered — no — Julie could *foresee* (it was hard to tell the difference between remembrance and foresight when you were just part of a daisy chain of mothers and daughters, of Liliths and Lamias) how she would do the same damn thing, tell the same story to a resistant daughter, who would maybe become a little less resistant over time.

It was hard to imagine Charles, who had once loved her docility and quietness, being or staying a part of that picture. Best to hide as much as she could from him.

Julie remembered and foresaw as she washed the dishes; she'd hung a crystal-and-brass suncatcher by the kitchen window and flakes of iridescent shadow wavered up and down her arms. Charles paced in the next room, describing two competing job offers to his parents over the phone. After their talk petered out, he rejoined Julie, dried the dishes she had already cleaned. He reported on the call, then asked, "So, what do you think? Where should we go next?"

Julie said it didn't matter — they could go anywhere.

So long as she had space for a garden.

*See M.E. Bronstein's story "Garden Teeth"
online at Metaphorosis.
If you liked it, leave a comment. Authors love
that!*

Remember to subscribe to our e-mail updates so you'll know when new stories are posted.

About the story

I'd say this story started with dragons' teeth before anything else. I've been intrigued for ages by Ovid's account of Cadmus sowing the dragon's teeth (which Charles alludes to briefly in the story), and the image of teeth-as-seeds just felt very dark and witchy, and so other associations started to spring up. That's often where stories begin for me, with weird images and chasing whatever connections feel intriguing. So, in this case: dragons' and serpents' teeth, dandelions (i.e., "lions' teeth"), and mythical women often associated with serpents, like Lamia and Lilith.

A question for the author

Q: What is your favorite fairy tale and why?

A: I always struggle with "favorites"! But I am a sucker for Beauty and the Beast and its assorted variants, especially Cupid and Psyche (the Crafts' gorgeous picture book was a major childhood favorite). As for why: that's a little difficult to articulate... but I'm often drawn to stories that capture something ambivalent about women's experiences, rather than insisting that they must be absolutely passive or agentive? Plus there's all the dense, very pretty symbolism. I also once taught a course on Beauty and the Beast and Bluebeard, as well as various retellings (broadly construed), and the unsettling ways the two story types can resemble each other.

About the author

M.E. Bronstein is an academic and creative writer who studies medieval translation practices and writes various kinds of horror and dark fantasy. Her very first short fiction publication appeared in *Metaphorosis*; since then her writing has also appeared in *Beneath Ceaseless Skies, PodCastle, khōréō magazine*, and elsewhere.

mebronstein.com

A word about Laurel Beckley

We first published Laurel Beckley on 22 October 2021, with her story "Tell the Crows I'm Home", about an older woman in rural Oregon trying to come to terms with a changing world. I loved the story from the moment I saw it — this was the kind of story *Metaphorosis* was created to house. If you haven't read it, you should put it at the top of your list. You'll be grateful you did.

Happily, Beckley also participated in our most recent original anthology, *Museum Piece*, a collection of stories about unusual museums. Beckley's story, "The Museum of Perpetual Service" offers a grim warning about the incentives that can pervert faith and loyalty into meaningless spectacle — but also about how to take charge of your own destiny.

Here, she's back in our pages with "But No Man Moved Me Till the Tide", a completely different story about embracing your true self despite pressure from others.

But No Man Moved Me Till the Tide

Laurel Beckley

Myrna met him on the bluffs above the cove after dinner.

It was a moonless night, the height of autumn. A night for sea monsters and storms. She closed her eyes, letting the presence of ocean wrap around her, as if she were the island being caressed by waves, as if she were swimming through the depths in her true form, currents whispering across her fur.

The wind whipped her curly brown hair, tickling and tangling while its icy touch nipped her exposed cheeks and ears. The approaching storm sat offshore still, kicking up the white-caps and pushing the stench of salt and fish guts and rain. It seemed like each year the storms arrived earlier and earlier, and with them the dangers of the deep.

Myrna opened her eyes. Fog enveloped everything but the piercing beam of the lighthouse above.

Flash. Four seconds. Flash.

She smelled Gabriel's human-musk before he crested the bluff. He was freshly shaved, hair slicked down with orange-scented pomade and wearing his nicest suit, which happened to be his lighthouse keeper's uniform. His hands, however, held his day's work embedded within each crease of skin.

"Hello, Miss Coates," Gabriel said.

His eyebrows bunched together as he eyed the pelt she carried in her arms, cradled like a child. She'd brought her pelt at her mother's insistence, tucking the grey-speckled fur so it resembled a jacket, the paws clenched tight in her fists so he could not wrest it from her. This was nothing like the uncivilized days when humans stole otterkin pelts and forced them onto land, but Myrna remembered the old stories. She didn't hand it over. Not yet.

As an otterkin, Myrna had known this moment would come. But unlike her cousins and older sisters, who'd spent their girlhood afternoons crafting scrapbooks and dreaming of the mysterious spouses who would arrive to bind the wild thing lurking inside all otterkin, Myrna had stared into the white-capped waves surrounding their island home. They'd grown up and found spouse-keepers, while Myrna had refused each human placed in her path. She'd always preferred the ocean to land. Her soft fur to pink flesh. And now her fate was here, in the form of her most persistent suitor, who would propose to her at any moment. He'd ask for her pelt and half her soul, and she'd have to obey, because that was what otterkin did.

Myrna clamped her lips tight to keep the brewing cry of refusal from erupting across the sea. The wild thing inside her scraped her chest, wanting out. Silence stretched between them, interrupted by the squawking of a gull.

"Would you like to walk along the ridge?" Gabriel asked.

Myrna nodded, not trusting herself to speak without screaming. She could do this—for herself, and for her family.

Gabriel was a kind man, a man who rescued jellyfish and fixed broken seagull wings and treated her younger cousins as children, but what person *wanted* an otterwife? A woman bound forever, a woman who was strong and loyal and could never leave, even in the most isolated of postings? A woman shuttered?

Their boots crunched sand and hallowgrass and rocks. Each step felt heavy as tradition and her family's increasing expectations weighed upon her, heavier than the cloudy night sky. Her family hadn't seemed to mind the loss of half of themselves. They had welcomed it with sighs of relief, as if they'd spent their whole lives waiting for the wild thing to be tamed. Her sisters would say she was lucky to have such a kind man wanting her. Her mother would tell her to stop protesting and submit, because this was as good as it got, and far better than she could have expected. But how would it change her, to give her soul to another's keeping?

Gabriel stopped at the trailhead leading down to the cove where her family swam each moon night, the only time their spouses allowed them to assume their true forms. Waves passed over the pebbled beach. The rocks trilled as the water ebbed back into the ocean, the sound rising through the fog.

"I know it's fast and we should have brought a chaperone, but we worked together all summer and I thought—I um, I want to do things proper, for you." Gabriel paused, fiddling with the lapels of his jacket. "My posting here ends in the spring. My next station is to the north, in Alanshaw. It's a single keeper position."

A single keeper with a spouse, if they had one. Without a spouse, he would be alone for the two-year tour. This was why he wanted a wife. Why he pursued Myrna.

It was a shame, Myrna thought, that she was the only one of marriageable age.

Gabriel bent, one knee resting on the rocks and sand, and looked up at her. Her breath caught. It was happening.

"Myrna, I—" Gabriel began, stretching a hand toward her.

His fingers brushed against her pelt. She jerked back from the touch, a lump clogging her throat, stoppering the scream, forcing it through her body instead of out, until she felt like she would explode if she didn't, if she—

"Myrna—"

His eyes were wide, pleading, the color of the ocean on a summer day, but reality was staring at her too and even though she was expecting it, she couldn't—*she couldn't give it up*. She took another step backward. Then another and another, one after the other, down past the rock outcroppings and the verbena and the sand as the waves crashed harder against the shore and the pebble-song screamed across the rocks and the storm wind picked up into a howl.

She ran until cold water kissed her shins, and then she wrapped her pelt about her shoulders and dove into the sea.

The fog and frigid water swallowed her whole, engulfing her in a harsh and angry and cold world as an undertow snagged her, dragging her down and down and down to the silt and rock bottom.

Myrna shed her boots with a kick, giving them to the ocean and shoving her feet into her pelt. She never swam in her human form—how ungainly, how slow, when she could be *majestic*.

Something brushed against the thick fur on her back. She yelped, spinning to catch the silvered flicker of a giant sea bass slicing into the deep. She twisted her body, hooking one paw around an algae frond as an anchor while she oriented herself, eyes adjusting to the dark.

She had been dragged further and faster than she had expected. She was no longer in the shelter of the cove, with its fields of coralline algae blooming in red and brown and mud-green, but had been pulled beyond the jetty, where the bottom dropped and the tall kelp grew. Where she was forbidden to go alone. Her heart hammered. She needed to get back to shore. To face—

Myrna did not know what fate waited an unwed otterkin. She'd only known of one. Eyde, who'd left the island when Myrna was a toddler and was only mentioned in whispered conversations among the oldest otterwives on winter nights when the shutters shuddered from the howling storms.

Myrna had broached the subject of not marrying once, and her mother had told her otterkin always wed because that was what was done, and that she'd better be quiet or the sea monsters would take her.

In marrying, an otterkin severed her ties to the sea and wildness and bound herself to humanity and civilization, and that was that.

Since she had turned eighteen, her mother had shoved men—and later, women and a few people who were neither man or woman—onto her daughter with increasing desperation and irritation.

None of her family understood Myrna's reluctance. They had been happy to give away their pelts, to set themselves firmly on land and a life of marriage and babies. They treated their monthly excursions to the cove as honoring their history, but while the sea was the source of their livelihood, it wasn't their life. It didn't sustain their souls, not like it did Myrna. She craved the wildness with a yearning she couldn't quite put into words. In the sea, she was free. She didn't want to give any part of herself away.

Myrna closed her eyes to stop her tears. The ocean didn't need more salt. She had to go home, and face her mother's disappointment.

She had taken only one stroke toward shore when she heard it.

The song rippled through the waves, soft and cooing. It came from beyond the tall kelp forest, the sound wending through the fronds and the stipes. Thoughts of her family, of Gabriel and expectation, fell away. Longing screamed through her, tearing away thought and reason and rationale and pulling all of her wants and desires just out of reach. The singer *yearned*, just as she did. There were no words, but she knew this desire, this need for something beyond…beyond. This desire to fill the hollow in her chest, to heal wounds scraped raw and bleeding.

The ocean's bottom plunged away as she emerged from the kelp forest.

Myrna kicked backward and grabbed a frond with her paws, the cold undercurrent threatening to sweep her into its depths.

The song faded. Myrna clutched the frond, straining to hear. The ocean was quiet and her heartbeat thrummed in her chest and her chest ached from the need for air and the song grew louder once again. The singer was right over there and —

The song turned sword-sharp and bloodthirsty as thick tentacle whipped up from the depths, spearing toward her.

Myrna screamed as another tentacle rose to join the first. She thrashed through the fronds, retreating through the forest toward shore as fast as her paws could pump.

Her vision greyed. Her lungs burned. She had to breathe.

She burst to the surface, and sucked rain-clogged air through her sharp teeth. The waves rolled high and vicious and the downpour of rain mixed with the tears streaking her fur-covered cheeks. When she caught her breath—she'd been in one place too long, far too long, surely the monster should have caught her by now— she plunged back into the water.

There was no sign of pursuit.

The monster had vanished, leaving only its song wending through the fronds of the forest, once again softly yearning, laced with such sorrow and regret that Myrna nearly swam toward it again. She fought the song, fear keeping her oriented to the shore. She swam the entire way without stopping, until she emerged onto the pebbled beach, never noticing the gills that had sprouted beneath her ears.

The storm raged about her as she cried and coughed the saltwater from her lungs. Her sobs mixed with the crash of waves and the howl of wind. She'd grown up hearing wintertime stories of sea monsters and the dangers of the deep waters. The past few years of winter storms had brought the sea monsters closer to the island, but there was ocean's breadth in the difference between hearing about a danger and facing it. Even on shore, she could feel the song echoing through her bones, and she did not know if her tears were of relief, or regret.

Not one of her family had ever said the sea monsters *sang*.

Gabriel kept up his courtship as if the night on the bluff had never happened, leaving flowers and a pink ribbon and a mewling grey kitten, as if the gift of a living creature would endear her to him. Myrna avoided him and hid her pelt in the carved space of a dead tree and tried to forget that the night of his proposal and the monster had ever happened.

Myrna heard the song again as she helped her youngest niece crack a mussel during their next moon night. She'd volunteered to watch the youngest girls, to teach them to pull their pelts about their shoulders, how to find the best rocks and tuck them into their foreleg pouches, how to surf the streams into the kelp meadow and forage for the tastiest sea urchins. She'd hoped that in teaching them she'd find that spark of motherhood, that desire for creation and nurturing that seemed to reside in everyone but her. Instead, she felt nothing but frustration.

The song was faint, and lonely, and before she knew it she'd drifted to the edge of the meadow and was between the first stipes of tall kelp. She pulled herself away—her otter limbs felt long and sinewy and strange—and dragged her niece to the surface, checking over her shoulder to see who else in her family was captured by the monster's siren song.

"Did you hear that?" Myrna asked her niece.

"Hear what?" the little asked, nibbling on a clump of seaweed.

A hiss nearby, from the cluster of teenage cousins floating in the middle of the cove. Their teeth bared in silent accusation for stringing Gabriel along when *they* would have been a much better match, if only they had been old enough to marry.

At the weight of their stares, Myrna pulled her niece to shore, fighting the song's pull with every stroke. No one else seemed to hear it. There must be something wrong with her, something that made her different enough to hear the sea monsters when no one else could. This difference scared her, because she didn't know what it meant.

As fall turned to winter, Myrna retreated into herself, avoiding her family as diligently as she did Gabriel.

She tried to ignore the gossip surrounding her, from her aunties, who gathered in clumps by the fireplace at nighttime, muttering, *Not like Eyde, no, not like her.* She tried to avoid her married cousins and sisters, but they sought her out while she was in the middle of her chores, telling her it was time to stop staring at the sea and get married to Gabriel already. They never said it outright, but she knew they thought it was past time for her to give her pelt into a human's keeping. Taming their wild thing was the civilized thing to do. As much as she dodged her cousins, Myrna couldn't avoid her mother, who just eyed her with a mix of frustration and pity.

Myrna bottled herself up, suppressing the wild thing that burned in her chest. She craved escape, but unlike before, when she could flee into the water whenever her family's expectations for her future became too much, now a sea monster waited for her in the depths.

She knew it was still there, because it stalked her.

Its siren song reached out to her on land, humming incessantly in her ears. The further she pulled from her family, the more the song tugged her, strumming along the tip of her tongue, leaving her irritable and filled with a yearning she could not explain because she did not have the words. It infected her soul, and she could not tell anyone because she didn't think anyone else had ever felt like she had before. Surrounded by her perfectly content aunts and cousins and sisters, Myrna felt like an island in a vast sea, besieged by fierce storms on all sides. It made sense that the sea monster targeted her. She was different. She was wrong. And the monster's song was her punishment for staying unwed and turning her back on tradition.

For keeping the wild thing inside her instead of giving it away.

Rain lashed the roof. Wind clawed the wood siding. The lighthouse's foghorn trumpeted, warning ships away. The monster's song shrieked above everything else, high and vicious and hungry.

Winter was sea monster season, when storms pushed the creatures closer to shore. This year was different. Four wrecks this month alone, each with survivors who spoke of tentacles wrapping about the masts, hurling their ships against the rocky shoals. The Head Keeper told his otterkin wife that he had never heard the ocean sing during a storm before, and she had told him it was just the wind over the rocks. But these stories brought the aunts together, whispers of *Eyde* and *never so bad before* and once, just when they thought she was out of earshot, *not Myrna.*

It was all a circle, from Gabriel chasing her to her aunt's outraged stares to her mother's sighs to her cousin's whispers to Myrna berating herself, asking what was *wrong* with her. Why couldn't she just say yes? Why couldn't she submit, like the rest of her family?

The monster's song changed, from vicious cry to sweet coo, warm and welcoming.

Myrna pulled her pillow over her head, trying to drown out thought and sound with goose down and cotton.

Her bedroom door banged open. "Abigail is missing," Myrna's mother said.

They rushed outside, Myrna urging her youngest siblings to stay *inside*. Her aunts and eldest cousins were already racing toward the cove, their white nightgowns clinging to their strong bodies, turning them into wraiths attacking the night.

Abigail was halfway down the beach when they found her, bent double and sobbing as she staggered toward the churning black water.

One of Myrna's aunts grabbed her arm, but the girl flung her off and was almost in the water when another aunt tackled her. It took all of them to hold the girl down, her eyes rolled white and her mouth open in a scream of need as her heels drummed the pebbled beach. Someone clubbed Abigail across the temple and the girl sagged. Her limp arms stretched toward the water, as if even unconscious she yearned for what the song promised.

Myrna stepped away from the thrum, rubbing her bloodied nose. She was on the verge of tears and didn't know why. The song caught her, its crackling desire meeting the wild thing inside, and she took three steps toward the water without even realizing it when the sharp sting of a slap brought her back to reality. Her oldest cousin grabbed her arm and dragged her back to her house, snarling that Myrna shouldn't have come, that this business was *married* women's work.

The aunties gathered at Myrna's mother's house that night, clustering about the hearth. Myrna boiled water for tea. She knew she wasn't allowed at this meeting, but she thought if she made herself useful and kept quiet she might learn why this was happening.

Myrna arrived with the tray right as her eldest aunt jabbed a finger at Myrna's mother and hissed, "Tell that girl to get her head straight and accept the boy already. We *cannot* have another Eyde."

She couldn't stop herself. "What happened to Eyde?"

Her aunts turned, their eyes dark and vicious, their teeth flashing otter-sharp from the light of the fire. "Go back to bed," her mother said.

Myrna fled.

Another storm hovered on the horizon.

Myrna grabbed her jacket from its peg by the door and left the house, ignoring her nieces' stares as they stopped flipping through last season's fashion magazine to watch her. Their whispers started the second her back was turned. Myrna wished they knew that she was just as scared as they were, that she didn't know why the storms were so bad this winter and why something lurked in the cove beyond the breakers. She wished they knew all these things, and yet she couldn't tell them, because speaking the words meant she'd have to admit she couldn't marry Gabriel, and to admit that meant that she was wrong and broken and the cause of everything.

She was the reason her family suffered. She knew she had to fix it, but she didn't know how. The only option she saw was unacceptable. Surely there was a way to keep her family *and* her soul? To keep herself for herself, and herself alone?

She walked straight to the shore without pausing to check her pelt in its hidey hole.

The waves were tall and vicious, sea foam whipping off the white caps and flying toward shore. The pebble beach's song screeched like hunting birds, even as the whisper of the sea monster's song caressed her cheek. Myrna wondered what it would be like to give in to the song, to dive into the waters. To sing instead of listen.

"Myrna?"

She turned away from the water. Gabriel stood at the top of the trailhead to the cove. His head bowed against the wind, his arms wrapped protectively around something the size of a winter jacket. Her stomach clenched.

He closed the distance the second he saw the horror on her face, thrusting her pelt toward her with both hands. "Your mother gave it to me."

Rain stabbed her cheeks, ice cold and spear-sharp. She didn't take the pelt. She couldn't move, couldn't speak.

So.

Her family had chosen for her, had gone back to the old days of pelt stealing. It was done. She had thought she'd feel *something*—that love her mother mentioned, or resignation or revulsion or anything at all, but her family's betrayal emptied her, excavating the wild thing that had lived inside her until she was a hollow shell.

Above her, the lighthouse beacon flashed. Four seconds. Another flash, cutting through rain and clouds and reminding her that anything she had wanted was just a dream—untouchable and nonexistent.

Words tumbled from his mouth, spilling like sea foam across the pebbled beach. "I really did want to wait. I had no choice. I'm being reassigned early." His hands clutched her pelt, his fingers smoothing and straightening it with as much gentleness as he had shown that newborn kitten. She'd given the kitten to a younger cousin, but she couldn't give this away. His voice dropped to a whisper, barely audible over the shrieks of the approaching storm. "I'll give it to you whenever you want, not just on moon days." He looked up at her, his face earnest. "I will love you. And you—you will learn to love me, too?"

As if she had any choice in the matter, anymore. "I will be whatever you wish of me, husband." Her voice was a croak, the word *husband* tasting like rotten fish in her mouth.

Hurt danced across Gabriel's eyes, and he tucked her pelt against his chest. It lay in his arms like a dead animal. He opened his mouth and took a step forward, but his eyes widened as he took in something behind her. "Oh, seas," he gasped.

Myrna turned to see what it was, and he grabbed her arm, jerking her toward him.

A fierce howl pierced the crash of waves. There was a flash above, the lighthouse slicing through the fog, and Myrna turned in time to see a massive tentacle lift out of the waves to wrap about the boulders at the edge of the cove. Another scream, a hunting song, angry and hungry.

The sea monster had come to shore at last.

Gabriel lunged for her. Myrna tried to sidestep him, tried to flee, but he grabbed her upper arm and whipped her around to face him. "No," he gasped. "I won't let you go."

Myrna stared into his eyes and saw her future unspool before her. Marriage and babies and expectation and all the things she could never do. Perhaps there would be pockets of joy and laughter with Gabriel, but she would never throw off the shroud of imprisonment. If she stayed, she would never refill the hollow inside her. The fear that had been building ever since that night in the kelp forest vanished, leaving only resolution.

The sea monster's song rose into the air, a triumphant battle cry, but she was not afraid. She did not want to die, but better that than the future that awaited her if she stayed with Gabriel.

He tried to pull her ashore, but she stepped away, jerking her pelt from his unresisting fingers. "I was never yours."

He did not reach for her again.

The song softened, the sea monster shifting away as Myrna took step after step down the uneven edge of the jetty. With the fog shifted, there was a woman standing at the end, wearing her nudity with the unconscious grace of an otterkin. And Myrna knew she *was* an otterkin, for despite her shark-sharp teeth and the kelp streaking her curly brown hair, she was the mirror image of Myrna's mother.

"I have grown tired of waiting for you, niece," Eyde said.

Myrna lifted her chin, trying to hide her confusion. "I thought the sea monster was here to kill me."

"There is death, and death." Eyde remained where she was, unafraid. "Did you ever wonder where the sea monsters came from?"

Myrna hadn't. Sea monsters had always existed, ruling the winter seas. "I don't understand."

Then she did. It was obvious, in retrospect. Sea monsters and otterkin were the same. She could not see through the fog, but she imagined Gabriel stood on shore still holding her pelt. Beyond him were her family and everything she knew. They were the ones who chose to bind themselves instead of embracing the wild thing that lived inside.

"They know, but they are afraid," Eyde said, her voice soft and gentle. "Why do you think they honor marriage and tradition as they do? But some of us cannot fit into their world, no matter how hard we try. And so we choose another way."

The lighthouse flashed above, its beam cutting through the fog, reminding her of the island and family and tradition. A wave crashed over the rocks, sea foam swirling about her legs, the ocean promising her adventure and a life bound to herself and the sea alone. Myrna was caught between sea and shore, but the hollow in her chest felt just a little bit less empty. Because for the first time in her life, there was a choice beyond what she'd always known.

Myrna turned back to her aunt. "There are more…people like us?"

"An entire ocean full." Eyde stretched out her hand in silent offer.

Freedom, but in exchange, she'd become a monster. She would lose her family, and everything she'd known. But she would gain herself. She would *live*. She would be among others just like her. Myrna glanced toward the shore one last time. And perhaps, eventually, she could return and make her own way back to her family. Both her, and the wild thing that lived inside.

She took her aunt's hand, and together they leapt into the sea.

See Laurel Beckley's story "But No Man Moved Me Till the Tide" online at Metaphorosis.
If you liked it, leave a comment. Authors love that!
Remember to subscribe to our e-mail updates so you'll know when new stories are posted.

About the story

The seeds of "But No Man Moved Me Till the Tide" started, oddly enough, in 2012 when I visited Chincoteague, VA. As a longtime fan of Marguerite Henry, I'd always wanted to visit, but surprisingly, the ponies were not the things that stuck out to me. I was intrigued by the Assateague Lighthouse (repainted since my visit), the isolation of the island itself, and also by a docent I met at the museum who was very kind—and who I didn't realize had written a book on the community of Chincoteague until I was at a bookstore an hour later and saw her name on one of the books.

However, the story itself was supposed to be a secondary world steampunk-ish fantasy novel about a journeyman lighthouse keeper who was 100% human. Because it had no plot, I stalled out at 45k words, and *The Keepers* has sat untouched on my computer since 2016. In 2021 I wrote a short story called "Terrible Tilly Hunts the Cadborosaurus" (*All Worlds Wayfarer*, Issue X), which resparked my thoughts of lighthouses, otter-shifters, and islands. In 2022, after reading a brilliant *Little Mermaid* retelling (I can't remember who wrote it) and feeling trapped by the anti-LGBTQ+ legislation being pushed throughout the US, I started playing around with a short story called "Otterkin", taking pieces of *The Keepers* and transforming it into a story about tradition, queerness (specifically, asexuality) and not fitting in with rigid societal expectations. I'd also been reading a lot of folklore about cryptids (specifically, animal-brides), which is where the otterkin people came from.

I tend to either know the titles of my writing right off the bat, or give it a working title like "Otterkin" or *The Keepers*, and then scour the internet for something in the public domain that catches my eye/fits the vibes of the story. "But No Man Moved Me Till the Tide" is a line from Emily Dickinson's poem, "I Started Early — Took My Dog".

This story took a lot of editing—I've ripped this story apart and pieced it back together more times than I can count, both by myself and with feedback from *Metaphorosis'* Morris and my short story writing group —to figure out what I was trying to do with this piece, to the point where the words stopped wording and my brain was no longer braining (this happens more often than you'd think). Many thanks to Morris, my writer's group, my wife and my friends. It really takes a village. Thank you, dear reader, for picking up this work out of the millions out there. And, museum docent Myrna, thank you most of all.

A question for the author

Q: Do you read more fantasy or SF (hard or soft)?

A: Both science fiction and fantasy are going through a huge renaissance right now, and it's just a great time to be an SFF reader. I'd love to say that I read both equally, but my reading spreadsheet reveals the lie. I read a lot more fantasy than science fiction, although science fiction is my favorite genre. I'm not really into hard sci-fi, although I will read it—I'm a mood reader to my core and I read a little of almost everything. The actual science and technology matters far less to me than political/social allegory, plot, character development and world-building, which is probably why I am a huge science-fantasy fan (the squishiest of soft sci-fi).

Since I'm a librarian, here are some recently-ish published favorites I recommend. Sci Fi: *Light From Uncommon Stars* by Ryka Aoki, *The City We Became* by NK Jemisin, *Gideon the Ninth* by Tamsyn Muir, *How High We Go in the Dark* by Sequoia Nagamatsu, *An Unkindness of Ghosts* by Rivers Solomon, *Some Desperate Glory* by Emily Tesh, and *All Systems Red* by Martha Wells. Fantasy: *Saint Death's Daughter* by CSE Cooney, *The Spear Cuts Through Water* by Simon Jimenez, *Jade City* by Fonda Lee, *The Bone Orchard* by Sara Mueller, anything by CL Polk, *The Dawnhounds* by Sascha Stronach, and *The Unbroken* by CL Clark.

About the author

Laurel Beckley is a writer, Marine Corps veteran and librarian. She lives with her wife, fur creatures, and a collection of gently neglected houseplants.

thesuspectedbibliophile.home.blog,
@laurelthereader

A word about Saleha Chowdhury

Usually, there's been quite a long wait between when I first add an artist to our roster for potential work and when I first call on them. But when Saleha Chowdhury first contacted us in 2018, I liked her work so much that I drew on her right away. Her cover illustration for Arlen Feldman's "Graveyard" was so good that I also chose it as the cover of the our 2018 *Best of Metaphorosis* issue — and there was very stiff competition that year.

I brought Saleha back almost immediately, for the February 2019 cover, illustrating Catherine George's "The Bear Wife". That cover, with a woman and child nestled inside a bear's open mouth, is still one of my favorites — as most of Saleha's work is.

She appeared again on the December 2019 (Laura Duerr's "What Lies in Light") and January 2020 (L. Chan's "Sonata") covers. That also makes her a member of the Meta4osis club — the select few that have appeared in *Metaphorosis* four times or more — and we've been very happy to have her!

In this volume, she provided the cover art based on M.E. Bronstein's "Garden Teeth".

You can find more of Saleha's work at www.salehachowdhury.com

About Saleha Chowdhury

Saleha Chowdhury is a digital illustrator based in New York who enjoys working on a wide variety of projects including cover art, background art for games, and character design. She especially enjoys working on projects related to science fiction and fantasy.

salehachowdhury.com, arodude.tumblr.com

Copyright

Title information

Metaphorosis Apr-Jun 2024

ISSN: 2573-136X (online)
ISBN: 978-1-64076-280-0 (e-book)
ISBN: 978-1-64076-281-7 (paperback)

Copyright

Publisher

Metaphorosis
a magazine of speculative fiction

Metaphorosis Magazine is an imprint of
Metaphorosis Publishing
Neskowin, OR, USA

www.metaphorosis.com

"Metaphorosis" is a registered trademark.

Discounts available

Substantial discounts are available for educational institutions, including writing workshops. Discounts are also available for quantity purchases. For details, contact Metaphorosis at metaphorosis.com/about

Metaphorosis Publishing

Metaphorosis offers beautifully written science fiction and fantasy. Our imprints include:

Metaphorosis Magazine
Plant Based Press
Verdage
Vestige
Joyful Heave

You can also find us:
@metaphorosis.bsky.social (Bluesky)
@Metaphorosis@writing.exchange
(Mastodon)
www.facebook.com/metaphorosis

Help keep Metaphorosis running by supporting us at
Patreon.com/metaphorosis

See more about some of our books on the following pages.

Metaphorosis Magazine

Metaphorosis
a magazine of speculative fiction

Metaphorosis is an online speculative fiction magazine dedicated to quality writing. We publish an original story every week, along with author bios, interviews, and notes on story origins.

We also publish monthly print and e-book issues, as well as yearly Best of and Complete anthologies.

Come and see us online at magazine.Metaphorosis.com.

Plant Based Press

Vegan-friendly science fiction and fantasy, including anthologies of the year's best SFF stories, from 2016-2020.

Chambers of the Heart

speculative stories
by
B. Morris Allen

A heart that's a building, a dog that's a program, a woman sinking irretrievably — stories about love, loss, and motion.

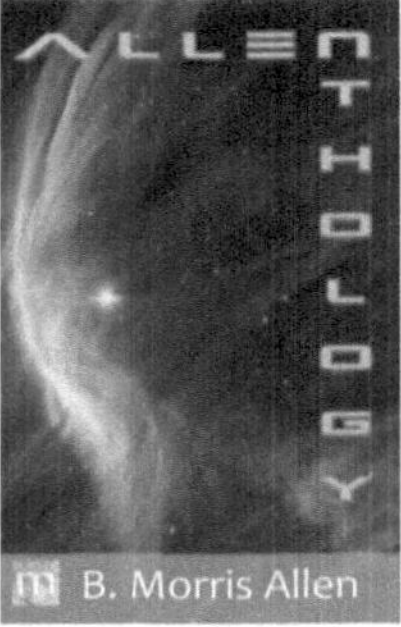

Susurrus

A darkly romantic story of magic, love, and suffering.

Allenthology: Volume I

Including three full collections of SFF stories.

Verdage

Science fiction and fantasy books for writers — full of great stories, often with an additional focus on the craft of speculative fiction writing.

Reading 5X5 x3

Changes

How do stories move from 'maybe' to published?

Here are 15 case studies of stories published in *Metaphorosis* magazine.

Reading 5X5 x2

Duets

How do authors' voices change when they collaborate?

A round-robin of five talented science fiction and fantasy authors collaborating with each other and writing solo.

Including stories by Evan Marcroft, David Gallay, J. Tynan Burke, L'Erin Ogle, and Douglas Anstruther.

Score

an SFF symphony

An anthology with an emotional score from the heights of joy to the depths of despair – but always with a little hope shining through.

Reading 5X5

Five stories, five times

See how different
writers take on
the same material.

Reading 5X5

Writers' Edition

Two extra stories,
the story seed,
and authors' notes
on writing.

Vestige

Novelettes, novellas, and novels by Metaphorosis authors.

The Nocturnals
Mariah Montoya

Night is Dangerous.
Day is deadly.

Where day and night last thirty years, humans move constantly stay ahead of the night and cruel Nocturnals that call it home. But a boy is lost out there.

Joyful Heave

Science fiction and fantasy anthologies with innovative and unusual themes.

Museum Piece
an unusual collection

A gallery of the strange and outrageous

Step right up and enter a world of wonder and oddities! These museums are not your typical tourist traps. From the Museum of Lost Dreams to the Suicide Museum, each exhibit will take you on a journey you won't soon forget.